Horizontal Hotel

A Nigerian Odyssey

D1413444

Horizontal Hotel
A Nigerian Odyssey

Richard Stevenson

TSAR
Toronto
1989

Cover art by Tony Partridge

The publication of this book is made possible with the
assistance of the Canada Council and the Ontario Arts Council.

ISBN 0-920661-11-4

TSAR Publications
P.O. Box 6996, Station A
Toronto, Ontario, Canada
M5W 1X7

Contents

I. Nonprescription Glasses

Third World Development As Depicted on a Tin of Mackerel

Open any book of nursery rhymes:
it's the cow that jumps over the moon.

We breathe molecules of Leonardo da Vinci.
Centuries too jump over their fences.

Count them. There are many names
for the fish caught in this parenthesis

of time and place. The label stays green.
The quick red fox jumps over the lazy

brown dog. Mackerel in tomato sauce:
perfect fish jumping unblemished red globes.

Ottawa Briefing

In Ottawa we walk the downtown streets at dusk.
African images pull up smart as late model cars
to vacant curbside slots of available thought.

Fat black squirrels stare blankly back from boulevards:
winter's consuls holding nuts between their paws,
metaphors unreal as MacKenzie King's crystal balls.

We stand and watch them stuff their cheeks,
beat it up the nearest beech. The generous plumes of
their tails trail blue-grey puffs of exhaust.

Our own accounts grow fat too: comic balloons
bearing five-figure digits like elevator passengers
or columns of mercury above fluffy white clouds.

We think of leaving the snow, of that first milk tooth:
the Rockies breaking through soft gums of white cloud.
Plane wing, a tongue depressor, presses down a big Ahh.

Kano Airport, The First Leg

Sky ferile, muscled with ominous intent.
To step onto the tarmac is to know immediately:
this is a greenhouse, heatsink of humidity.

Republic or loose confederation of states:
it matters little, signifies less.
Our thoughts' tiny fish mouth their meniscus.

Too much thought and too little time
to slip a lozenge past the broken teeth here;
sleep slides sluggish as slave ships into

the bight of mind, while blades of the fans
stand stiff as soup spoons in a horizontal broth. Moths smash
themselves against windows and walls.

Locusts crunch underfoot. Khaki is not a uniform,
but a state of mind: for this could be Havana
as Hitchcock or Greene might have imagined it,

and they would have got it wrong. The heart of
the matter is not in the manner or metier of
the people: a pulse taken with two fingers

on a wrist. Chevrons sit on the shoulders
as uneasily as the vultures sit in the trees.
Bats careen to the cacophanous dips of some

invisible conductor's own manic baton.
Signs say, "Do not spit on the floor or walls."
The eyes of the customs officials say it better:

Wind down white folk. There are no tourists here.
Politicians have rolled dung balls of foreign aid
across this plane before. The eyes of the mantis

give back the light. The light here is a long
shallow grave in which white sails billow out,
slip silently away. We have been where you go.

Billboard Sign, Maiduguri

"Feed well, grow strong":
words as ethnic, plebeian
as the bricks that go into
houses in the new G.R.A.*;

as obvious as "You Tarzan, me Jane"
in the sad, ironic way
they mock Madison Avenue
patterns of syntax and stress.

The smile and dress, the palmaded hair
of the chocolate girl that wears them
belie the kwashiorkor bellies of
children playing in the dust below.

"Feed well, grow strong":
eat our macaroni.

* Government Residential Area

Tender Lion Steak

Befuddled, I confront the Lake Chad menu.
So many exotic delights to choose from...
What shall I order today? Jellof Rice? Egusi stew?
Hmmm...When in Rome they say...
My keening eyes alight on a main course I've never had:
Tender Lion Steak. An interesting irony that, not so?
The King of Beasts gets eaten by good old Homo sapiens.
(Yet another depleting resource? In the Sahel no less—What would Joy
Adamson say? Marlin Perkins? Jane Goodall?)
Confronting damage done, I decide to order anyway.

Sannu, Mallam, I begin, deferring politely to the waiter.
Yauwa, sannu, the waiter replies, and does a soft shoe,
adjusts the dirty towel draped dextrously over his arm.
Abi you go order am now, mastah? (Ah yes, pidgin...
Let us not confuse a bird in the hand with regional dialect,
I think. He speaks English, by God. So much for Rome,
rudimentary Hausa. Enough small talk. Bring am de chop.)
Yes, well, this looks interesting. I'll have your lion.

Sah? Mallam waiter inquires of me. Disting?
And lays a black spatulate finger on the menu entree.
Yauwa, I reply. I've never had lion before.
Is it good? Does it taste anything like beefsteak?
Sah, is beef. E come from de cow. Small small cow.
I tink you sabe, abi? You bature eat am plenty beef.
E na be so? You go like am. I go get am for you now?
Ah! Tender loin! Bature sabe. Yauwa! Please, yes...
Bring on the beef...And a salad for madam.... Two star.
Madam is coming. She's just putting on her makeup.

Flying Coffins

It is forty degrees. To walk is to arrive
exhausted, beat before my white chalk
reaches the board. Fat cells melt like wax.

The ass of my pants sag slack sails
ahead of the mast that first dragged
white boys to this harsh grave of light.

I hail a van: Toyota Hi-Ace.
Haggle calmly over the price.
Shiga, the man says, meaning: enter.

I smile and take a back seat,
enter the country the way a foreign
substance enters the blood.

Maiduguri Market

1.

Not a department store
(though it might as well be),
but a maze of tin shacks,
muddy alleys, rickety tables.

Burlap awnings, large umbrellas
protect the well-to-do from sun;
the rest pile fruit like cannonballs
at strategic entrances, exits,
busk for business, or pick pockets.

You can drop your wallet here
and someone will return it;
pick it from another's pocket,
the proprietors will gang up
and beat you to death.

2.

Nothing has a set price, of course.
Yet the best shoppers among the batures
are not the most calloused, the most indifferent,
nor are they the ones that learn Hausa
or develop the best pidgin patter;

they are the ones that arrive early—
before the threat of a lean day's wages—
or the ones that arrive late—
for whom quality and need of purchase
scarcely matter, since the larder is not bare.

They are the ones that are not squeamish
and can discern difference between
one flayed piece of beef and another
between strokes of the horse-hair whisk
that alights like a wand scattering flies
first from one raw chunk, then from another.

Those who stretch a naira note know:
a white skin is the ticket to start low.

3.

Everything has a respectable low—
bargain basement prices that
frequently bottom out below cost
when produce threatens to perish
or a lead item can lead to a close
on something else, some other time.

In that way a white skin
is as good as a Chargex card.

The locals think we batures are rich:
and it is true; we are—in advantages
if not wages (We can afford to
"dash" authorities, and can choose not to).
We can leave; we can get out:
it is a truth of hard currency,
a bond as negotiable as beauty or sex.

Sannu, Bature*

Van is from Guyana and black
as any man in this market place.
So why do they call him bature, he asks.

We, his white soul mates, laugh,
tell him to be thankful that
they do not call him Oreo.

It's your keening eyes, man. The way
they light upon the glitter of their wares.
Those Pepsodent pearlies give back the light.

Flaunt a little Hausa, trim the sails
of your Western clothes; all inroads
lead to the dying embers of your eyes.

So say sannu back; you're black, man,
black as any pupil shrinking from the light,
but, oh, your soul, Van; your soul is white.

* literally: "Hello, whiteman" in Hausa.

The Pink Teacher

First day back from the University Primary School you tell me of the children in your charge: how their teeth gleam a whiter white than even God might have made the Pearly Gates. Or how they brandish the blood-red sign of ferrets in your henhouse. "Cola nut does it," you say. A stain, not unlike the stain of coffee. A richer buzz in the nut.

They are all black, save one or two expatriate Indians: and they are browner than you will ever be, no thanks to Chloroquine, the ashen grey of prophylaxis against malaria: bad air they thought once, when whites were snuffed as easily as the votary candles. And now you breathe in deeply. Take in "leper bits" with the usual furies the Harmattan brings.

But you are not white to them. Their powers of perception—if not their knowledge of Western painters' palettes—are more discriminating. The black men are not black, but black, brown, yellow—depending on the amount of melanin, the richness of the patina your camera will not dispense to you. You are not white, but pink: soft as a hand-washed shirt, a box of wax crayons left out in the sun. Colours run. You genuflect before the bleeding prints, offer them only the white wafer of your words. White is a figure of speech, you say.

Nonprescription Glasses

Nonprescription, Haruna says,
but not without purpose:
a man in glasses has status.
The Hausa man believes he is
a man of importance, position;
the white man's glasses have power.

Wear a pair of glasses
and a Hausa man will sit up
and take notice. Things'll get done.
Yes, you'll be treated with respect.
Baba riga, hula,* and glasses:
the glasses don't have to fit.

* voluminous gown and cylindrical hat:
formal dress in northern Nigeria.

Almajiris, Kashim Ibrahim Road

In the shadows of the neem trees
the almajiris sit, stitch
hours of daylight into their hulas
prismata of prayer, Islamic lines.
So many rows, coordinated to match
the well-lined pockets of the Alhajis'
baba rigas, bridgework of Hajj.
So many combinations, permutations
of the same basic design:
cylindrical hats on wooden forms
lined up like pistons
at the side of the road
sit beside abandoned
engine blocks billboard of sky.
Lizards fix you with limbic looks
nod like politicians run up a tree.
The almajiris chant Arabic:
syllables' exotic bees
worrying the bruise of their fallen fruit.
"Bature! Teacher! Come! Bring money!":
words bitten once discarded oxidize
the white wound of their smiles.

Sabon Tasha Bus, Maiduguri

Above the welded cages of the taillights two exotic butterflies, left and right, displayed as collectors' specimens; the words "Fear God" or "Nagode Allah" hand-painted like a field of daisies between them. "Prayer Is Telephone To God" emblazoned across the sliding side door; Nescafe, Cafenol, and Maggi decals all over the windows. You almost don't notice the two yellow blotches for bungy cords and page girls pouting and primping, spilling out of their naughty-Hollywood poses. You think of *Vargas, Playboy*: the hard sell at home. Images thankfully not plastered everywhere here, when the hyena-like camouflage dissolves, the purdah of Harmattan is dispersed; you see them: upside-down silhouettes of Africa proudly displayed. Do they not know you wonder—or does truth only slide like spittle from the glass? What religion then? What technology to hold these two yolks spilling out of their shells?

The Child's Head

The child's head has been shaved,
looks like the pocked surface of another planet,
where men might leap a hundred feet
in almost zero gravity.
Flies, seen from a distance as spots,
might be a herd of lunar ruminants
stopping at the neighbourhood waterhole.

But there are no Bambies
drinking the cool waters of their reflections here,
nor will the language of this place scab over.
The fly that drinks from the child's eye
drinks freely. The child stares
through his own telescope
at the moon of my white skin.
Doesn't raise a finger, doesn't blink.

"I'd Like To Connect Your Acquaintance..."

We laugh about it now.... Picture poor Adisa bringing his battered cab to a halt outside the big blue gate.... Broken glass snarling from the cement gumline of our housing compound fence.... Running round to your side to let you out—the perfect gentleman but for the imperfections in his English.... Only he had ulterior motives it seems...in retrospect... No doubt he had a particular coupling in mind. Bayonnet mount, like that joining camera to lens...quick, easily detachable.... And it's true, in the course of a half-hour journey, he had your name and address, knew where to come back to...a week, two weeks later, having watched for you whenever you left work so he could be Johnny-on-the-spot.... Had managed to appeal to your pride by convincing you he wanted something better for his children..."You... teacher...you go teach am English proper, abi?" Free rides for you, a few extra naira to take his kids off his hands for a couple of hours...teach them what cups and saucers and utensils were...how to use a European toilet.... Only he went straight to De Beer Parlour Hotel in Wulari ward, arrived later, more rancorous each night to pick them up...angling for something.... Finally, spelled it out: You could keep the children, take them to Canada with you...maybe bring them back...later, when they spoke perfect English. It would be no problem with mom to take her pickanin-o, oh no! mom worked very hard too...and she had two other young ones to help her at the kiosk.... Canada would be good for them.... They would be good.... You could bring them back any time you wanted to....

Tribal Scars

Wide-wale welts (a la corduroy)—one dead center from forehead to chin (over Nilotic, aristocratic nose); two others, parallel to this, on either side...or three quick nicks —parallel, horizontal—cat whiskers, a hair off the corner of the lips. Some triangular, dyed blue, mid-cheek— almost suffice as dimples or beauty marks.

They frighten, intimidate we white boys, at first...to think of the will of any parent to cut his child in such ways...to do so without sterile instruments in the worst of conditions, with the most caustic powders... and for what? Identification? A ritualistic mask?

I think of hair shirts, Christian novices flailing themselves for the rush hyperventilation and asepsis provide...the numinous moment of release when the stone is known with stone intelligence...the senses are keen as the lash of a whip.

Is it for this? The reminder of a birthright that antedates the white presence here?

I have heard it said the practice derives from the necessity of recognizing fellow tribesmen in time of war, or during the slave trade...that rank and privilege are somehow involved...

But what scar is this that issues blithely from the talking head's lips, courtesy of the local network T.V.?

I have been told this woman is paralyzed from the neck down. Yet from her lips comes the lash, the sting of a steady stream of the Queen's English. B.B.C. received pronunciation no less.

She looks straight into the camera. Perfect parallel waves slice through the air... insinuate themselves...a bouquet of flowers in the flared bell of our history's misbegotten blunderbus.

Health Science Class

You have moved on to physiology,
consider the response of the iris
to sudden changes in light intensity.

The children stare into each other's eyes,
wait for some miraculous change to take place
when they take away the heels of their hands.

The experiment is stymied by the fact
that black pupils seen against black irises
aren't as clear as white lines on a blackboard.

So you cover your own eyes in a kind
of see-no-evil parody or monkey shine
while your black pupils constrict around you.

There is a hush, a sudden gasping for breath
when you quickly withdraw your hands
and the blue tide of the facts rushes in.

The susurration of voices that follows
is older than the murmur of Lake Chad's
shrinking shoreline. Leaves something brighter

than two blue bottle shards there
in the alluvium of your lesson plan.
You feel yourself being sucked into

deeper water with each inhalation
of their communal breath; are released
with each sigh, flash of their polished teeth.

Their laughter is implosive, erodes
your knowledge with a silence louder
than the clatter of white beach stones

clambering, tumbling over one another
at the rim of your world, for here
meaning is meat scraped clean of the bowl.

Shit Alley

Hardly a thoroughfare—
a gulley, culvert really,
and aside from the privacy
afforded by a ten-foot drop
from the railway tracks,
almost totally exposed,
glared at by the sun.

A few giant milkweed bushes,
their green scrotum pods
proudly displayed,
seem to be engaged
in the most natural
of functions themselves.

And yet this is it:
the public convenience
where the locals "ease themselves."
An eroded hollow of discarded
car bodies, engine parts,
among which grow
toilet-paper blossoms
like puffed cotton bolls.

Following the laterite track
from Bolori to Wulari
along the railway line,
I pass this place every day—
have to—to catch a cab
along the Baga road.

And every day I greet
the locals hunkered there
for their constitutionals.
"Sannu," I say and try
to keep up a brisk pace.
And , politely, they reply.
This a kind of gauntlet
that teaches me to withold my own
moral nuggets of reproof and disgust.

Building Conditions

Every expat has a story
about the day he moved in:
the drainboard of a kitchen sink
isn't set into a countertop
and functions as the cabinet top
while the sides are made of
poorly painted quarter-inch plywood;
termites have caused a false
ceiling to sag and collapse;
the curtain valence
wedged between two walls
shrank and fell on the company
while madam was pouring tea;
it took three days
to chip the mortar from
the bathtub where the workers
mixed it to grout the tiles.
One expat even found
human excrement in his!
A door swings the wrong way,
won't swing past the toilet
to give a man his privacy.
Everyone has stories,
and almost everyone adjusts—
life is so tough, after all,
for the man with a roof
over his sunburned white pate,
and whether the roof is tin
or tile or straw,
or the rooms are air-conditioned
or afforded with fans
(depending what degree or shingle
a man has hanging on his wall,
what step and increment
the government has offered
on the state salary grid
to retain his services),
the terrazzo is cool,
the walls are firm
and keep the rabble out.

How To Get To Sleep in the Hot Season

First, forget the bottom sheet:
a terry towel is what you need.
Next, turn the ceiling fan on five
to keep the mosquitoes off your hide.
Then take down the mosquito net
(Pray they haven't got in yet).
Next, check the air viscosity
and adjust the fan's velocity.
(Pray the blades don't then decide
to drop off their bolts on "liquify.")
Then take the top sheet in the shower.
(Repeat as necessary each half hour.)

II. No Condition is Permanent

Expatriate Stories

Barry, the British structural engineer,
likes to tell the one about the time he
and a friend were walking to the club.

A van passed by and two men shoved
another, bound, trussed, out the side door.
His throat was slit. What could they do?

Syl recounts the one about two thieves in Lagos
who beat up a Pakistani for not wearing a watch
for them to steal. (He bought one the next day.)

Ed likes to warn the new boys not to stop
if they ever hit a pedestrian. Some peasants
stoned a bature to death when he stopped to help.

John warns present company not to stop a thief.
One Polish fellow did. The thief's cohorts
came back and cut him to ribbons.

The penalty for armed robbery is death,
so life is cheap, he explains. Luckily, a team
of expat doctors were able to patch our man up.

And so the stories go: robbery, death, mutilation
topping the list of favourite horror hits.
The new boys' faces grow whiter in the moonlight.

All nod like neems lovingly attended by the
domestic gardeners: trees that grow too leggy,
too heavy to support their own weight.

You get drunk fast in a climate like this:
More water evaporates through your pores
than you can ever hope to piss away straight.

No Condition Is Permanent

1.

The first time I read this slogan
I was in a battered Peugot 504 cab.
The driver was hell-bent on passing
an oil-spewing, dented wreck ahead.
He kept up a steady tattoo on the horn
and deked in and out of traffic,
prayer beads swinging to the juju
blaring from a torn tweeter in the dash.

A bungy cord hooked through the hole
where the trunk keyhole used to be
and wrapped twice around the bumper
kept the lid on a villager's goat.
We bumped up and down potholed streets,
through the Igbo quarter of Gwange ward,
and passed that cab riding the soft shoulder,
two wheels on the pavement, two wheels off.
The sign was emblazoned on a bus that nearly
sideswiped us into an open sewer alongside us.

I remember thinking the words were
a kind of moral equivalent to the bumper
snicker back home. I smiled, but complacently,
for I knew that, despite the constant bleating,
the terrified rolling eyes of the goat
that would have its throat slit come Sallah,
I and my White Anglo Saxon Protestant ass
would soon "get down" on good old terra firma too,
and I would only be a few kobo
lighter in the purse, and no worse for wear.

2.

That was when the moral imperative hit home.
I know better now. The camera and binoculars
I used to wear casually around my neck
while strolling out my front door and off
across the fields of guinea corn, thorn trees,
baobab are gone—as are half my clothes,
the local crafts pieces and objets d'art

I used to decorate the mortared cinder
block walls of my pastel pink home.

Now the broken glass bottles embedded
in the cement gums of the housing compound,
the new burglar bars in my lovely latticed
French windows and doors, a dog I feed
better than most of the local people eat
make a kind of sense to me. Like it or not,
I'm a prisoner in my home, and the condition
has become endemic, taxing my white bretheren
still living in Maiduguri. Batures all:
"European persons," no matter what country
we call home; none of us are tourists here.

On the Road to Benisheikh

for Haruna Timta

As though these were merely bystanders,
country squires rubbing shoulders,
the two fat jacks in the middle
were police officers in uniform,
the next two, reporters
in khaki raincoats and fedoras;

as though this were a fifties movie—
black and white—a bad print
full of blips and snow and flux;
the men with the cue cards for the next
commercial break were standing in the wings
to show us how to wash away the stains;

as though the camera had teeth
corn-kernel perfect, whiter than white,
and smiled back like dentures in a glass;
this celluloid wafer we genuflect before
was brought to us courtesy of
some major network sponsor;

as though our car could slip down
the dark throat of this day
as easily as a candy-flavoured lozenge;
the horizon might fly up suddenly
like a window blind at the end
of the first or second reel;

these vultures perched on the back
of a dead Fulani cow
hold footage of evolution
up to the light, rethread
the take-up reel from sun to moon,
play back the flight of pterodactyl to petroleum;

show us a land where no one
has book, bib, or prayer
cleaner than the sun's,
where each frame is bleached,
content leached sooner than the soil's,
and words melt quickly on the tongue.

Rosy Guest Inn, Zaria

—after Wole Soyinka's "Telephone Conversation"

"I'm sorry, sir,
we only rent rooms to ladies"—
straight face, no ironic smile—

you'd swear he'd been
trained at one of the best
hotel schools in London or Paris,

only this is Zaria:
fish wink from tins
in trash heaps and puddles.

I smile at the euphemism,
assuming that is what it is—
he is so straightforward, so honest—

means: no room in this inn
for a husband and wife team,
no dey come here for sleep—

not Christian, not Muslim.
If you've got a donkey or car,
you park it out back.

Taking Pictures Is Dangerous

This one's too good to miss:
backdrop of coconut palms,
banana trees, tall green grass;
silver bridge spanning
a slow-moving river.

The sun glistens,
gives back a surface
of roughly tooled brass.
I brake. You roll down
the window and focus.

But the boy, bewildered at first,
is finally firm: "Non, non."
He hides the iguana
he was holding by the tail,
backs off as if your camera were a gun.

Nor can you cajole him into posing
with a smile or cadeau
of a few hundred francs.

The country broke twenty-five French governors
in fifty years of colonial rule
you later discover
when looking for a clue.

Now governments change quicker
than you can change
the shutter speed.
Maybe, if you'd bought the lizard to eat...

—Grand Popo, Benin

Two Fly Whisks

In a glass case they sit:
candy apples on sticks:

two human skulls,
mandibles afixed in grim tiaras,

horse hair blossoming
from new fontanelles:

Portuguese soldiers
killed by the Fon:

fly whisks for
the Dahomean king.

Our guide speaks French.
We remember a little—

a few words,
flies behind glass.

                    —Abomey Museum, Benin

Horizontal Hotel

In stark, white letters
against a green background,
the words proclaim it:
the antinomies of life and death
acquire a title and deed.

Whorehouse or morgue?
The words take off their clothes,
Eden-rich with temptation;
we laugh, tell ourselves
to come back with a camera;

take note of the slogans,
hyperbolic extensions
of Madison Avenue chic;
laugh at the naivity in
street advertising technique:

"Prayer Is Telephone To God,"
"Man Must Wack Food Hotel,"
"The One Great Hitler's
Famous Photo Studio":
invariably the same tin shack:
a temporary filling
in a mouth of bad teeth.

We sidestep the puddles,
putrefying fruit,
tin cans and trash;
shower the moment we get home.
Exhaust and Harmattan dust
wash off easier
than truth and disease.

Hell, our people invented soap,
and when there wasn't enough
phosphate or perfume,
we had an answer
for that too.

Hoopoe

Strange crested bird
riding a thermal now
over burning grass

you flap flap flap
to gain altitude
As soon lose it

drop gently
peak to trough
in a perfect

sine curve
of this country's
vital signs

Catch
as catch can
whatever mote

whatever insect
spikes your need
and mine

find meaning
in this soft
pink pastel of dusk

Baobab to baobab
thorn tree
to thorn tree

Weave a kind
of thread
through it all

Leave the moon
that pale grub
impaled on a thorn

while the sun
a broken calabash
spills libations

to the
West.

Dead Dog

A plush toy,
legs stiff, tipped on your side,
you seem more of a mastiff
in death than in life;

bloated by maggots,
putrescence, and heat,
loaned the dignity of a snarl
where the skin atrophies
away from your teeth;

chained to the bones
of an old Peugeot
scrapped a hundred feet
from the side of the road
near De Beer Parlour Hotel;

so much different
from the Giacometti hobo
you might have been last week,
nosing through the garbage heaps.

Your brothers and sisters
will rip the soft underbelly of the moon,
leave it glistening like fine bone china
when they find you here.

And for a few days,
when the neighbours come
to defecate, they too
will notice the smell.

Agamas, Lake Chad Hotel

Sitting under the thatched umbrella
of a table in the patio bar,
I notice they are everywhere,
timid, skittish at first—
rather like squirrels
skittering about the patio stones.

I want to throw them some nuts,
but they eat flies
and there are plenty of these
landing, refueling, taxiing
along the walls and cinder blocks
to keep them in chop
for as long as they care to eat.

Those that have already dined
seem distant, haughty somehow.
Remind me of Ella Fitzgerald's
disdainfully delivered line:
"Miss Otis regrets
she cannot lunch today."
Perhaps it's the way
they lead with their chins,
like the famous caricature
of Truman Capote in *The New Yorker.*

After they check me out,
see I'm no more threat than a chaise lounge,
they dance to a different tune,
"Lounge lizards in heat,"
zoom up and down the walls,
tree trunks, table legs, over my feet.

Soon the whole place has become
a convoluted series of clover leaves
in a rich kid's toy roadrace set.
I want to yell, "Stop!" Take the remote control
and send them skittering off the track in one great
fireball—a fifty-car pileup at the end of the patio,

but no: that'd only bring on the skinks like so many
stretcher bearers—medics deking in and out of the flames.

So I sip my beer in peace and watch this Indianapolis
of leaping lizard hormones; give them the checkered flag
to chirp and smoke their scaley tires where they will—
even come to enjoy the pure ecstacy of it—
my heart pumping like a kid in the stands,
for they're not like squirrels after all,
with their quick ditch and recovery of seed,
but more like a quick replay of the dinosaurs
on a miniature set. And suddenly the guests
seem somber and slit-lidded by comparison.

I want to say, "O.K., fellow mammals, let's all copulate
and pile atop each other like a wrecking yard
of old car bodies in heat. Let's really cheat time
and get down to the funk of fossil fuels,
each molecule of our being slipping past the next
like a greasing of palms. Let's get down and hump,
even now while this one quizzical fellow, this old
English schoolmaster of a patriarch looks on in disbelief.

Chins up, wattles wagging while our carotids
strain against the stiffness of our starched shirts,
while old Darwin here cocks his head quixotically—
as though listening for his master's voice—
let's let him know we're not like the poor kid
in the back row who dared to fart during roll call.
Then, detecting nothing of an impertinent noise,
this staunch fellow too can return to the class
register to begin the roll call again."

Dancing at The Askill Club

The rules are simple:
"No bathroom slippers,
no gay dancing,
no dancing alone. "

And here we are:
one homosexual male
Canadian farm boy,
& one heterosexual on the make.

So now what?
The only single women
are prostitutes
(a hidden agenda
in one of the rules).

Our Queen of Gashua is cool
(gold chain, slacks, real shoes),
gets out on the floor anyway,
while I sip my brew,
make eye contact with a prostitute.

No sooner am I up,
than, sure enough, the D.J.
pipes up on the P.A.,
"No dancing alone!"
My friend, the only other
white man on the floor,
points at himself & replies,
"Who, me?" then shrugs,
slinks off the floor.

No one's caught my dancing slippers
(thongs in Canadian parlance):
perhaps because they're not
the thin plastic kind.
So I'm good for one woman, one dance.

Then the Queen decides to play straight,
works one side of the dance floor,
while I work the other.
And this is the way the evening goes:

One woman, one dance,
until the pimps know
neither of us is buying.
They shut us down: no dancing allowed.
We move on to the next bar.

Nightly Ritual

First, I shut the windows.
Each with its noodle-thin
horizontal-vertical lattice
of cheap spot-welded steel,
bendable enough for any adult
to get his child accomplice past.

Next, I lock the French doors.
Find the right latch key first,
then fit the padlock through
the new inside loops.
Then bathrooms, study, livingroom,
kitchen, watercloset, hall:

Ten minutes flat to make my rounds.
You might think I was the night
watchman or a company janitor,
miguardi for some rich Alhaji
away on business and not
expected back for weeks.

But no: this is my home—
laid on as part of my job.
I pay a paltry fifty naira,
while the college pays a thousand
to lease the place for me from
some Muslim businessman.

Yet I draw the drapes so as
not to advertise the few
sticks of furniture I have.
Pay a miguardi to sleep
with a quiver of poison arrows
on a prayer mat outside my door.

Paranoia? I hope so,
though last week my Nigerian
neighbours came home
to find a necklace of blood
girdling their miguardi's neck,
not so much as a sheet to cover him.

Last details then: my watch,
glasses on the night table;
below my pillow, a knife;
under the bed, a length of pipe;
on the floor, within easy reach,
a box of matches, jar of gasoline.

Why Does It Cry So?

Why does it cry so? Mohammed asks,
our electric iron sputtering, spewing
water in his hand. Why does ours cry
when his doesn't? I think: electricity,
heating coil, boiling water, steam.

How marvellous that he should be
so ignorant of this thing we take for granted;
how exciting to be able to see
God's mysterious ways working
the creases into my pants.

How sad that Mohammed
should feel the compunction to be
so god-damned polite in asking us
if he could use ours to iron his.
We feel embarrassed and humbled too

that ours should have such a forked tail
and depend on such transfusions
as the god of electricity will allow.
How far the cord has really stretched
that we should find our shirts
floating like kites with so many keys
attached.

Rinse Cycle

A picture of maternity
such as Grandma Moses
might have painted it:

Knitpurl, knitpurl, pause:
madam puts down her knitting,
bends to her steward an ear—

almost like the RCA Victor
pooch before the Victrola
listening for her master's voice.

Scrub, scrub, swish—yes,
it's the laundry all right,
but the intermittent flush?

She gets up to check,
and sure enough: Sale's
discovered a better way

than the grape-squashing,
knees-up-Mother-Brown
method in the tub.

Almost listening itself,
the porcelain ear of the toilet
receives her episcopal shirts.

Robbed!

Open the livingroom door on return from anywhere:
the facts of the deed like cockroaches scurry away.

Wedding suit, tape player, camera; the works!
Only the missing suitcase is big enough to contain the hate.

We're thirsty now and all there is is the sickle moon:
the handle of a broken teacup with which to toast the sun.

Someone points out that we'll have less to pack. We laugh.
What else can we do without binoculars to stuff the scenery in?

It's like that sometimes. Clouds like so many white shirts
enact their dance-of-the-hollow-sleeves. The wind is never

cooler than the bones it fails to reach. We're left with
the long line of horizon, a few trees to peg down the sky.

Testing, One, Two...

I'm feeling cocky today.
It is the tenth time in two weeks
I've come to see the deputy of police
about the official theft report I need
to file for insurance back home.

"Testing, one, two, three," I repeat
into the contact microphone
of the new portable cassette recorder
I have hidden between books
in my handy knapsack.

"Testing, one, two, three," the angry
magnetized syllables snap back
over the finely-honed heads.
"Heh heh. I've got you now, mother—,
I've got you—, I've got—, I—"

This is the day. Tomorrow 'e come,
I think, mopping my high brow,
and another fly takes off from
the short runway of my lips,
strafes the front windshield with shit.

This is it. Lie all you want, guys;
the commissionaire is Igbo by tribe,
not Kanuri, not Bura, not Hausa.
(Sweat beads line up like torpedoes
in the fine-grained bays of my pores.)

I step out of my car, abandon
it as the hermit crab does his shell, once
a newer, more secure home is found.
Say hi to all the black guys nodding
over files behind the front desk.

"The D.P.O. is off at the hospital
having a meningitis shot, you say?
That's nice.... I'm sorry, but I didn't
catch that. You'll have to speak louder...
You'll have to speak louder—, You'll—, You—"

Torturing Them Proper

Chi has become a good friend.
He is reliable, trustworthy, honest—
and, yes, thankfully, not
a domestic I have employed.

He lives in my "boys quarters"
because he asked if he could.
He is an Igbo, studies accounting,
has run south for his life before.

(Some still regard him as Biafran,
as pariah—my steward, for example,
who lives the thickness of a wall away
and still calls him "that Igbo man.")

And, anyway, nepotism, tribalism
in this town will assure
any available Hausa-owned housing
will go to a Hausa man first.

Had he anything to gain by trusting
in my white hide to shelter him
from prejudice; had I hired him,
he would still be my friend.

And so I believe him when he
shows concern at my being robbed.
I trust in his knowledge of back doors
in dealing with a corrupt police force.

And when he is delighted at a prospect
and tells me he has good news,
I am delighted too. I lean into
his words as a neem leans into sun.

I am hopeful when he tells me
the police have apprehended two thieves.
Am overjoyed to learn of a secret cache
of stolen goods found in my neighbourhood.

I can go down to the lockup right now,
see if anything there belongs to me,
and for a moment I allow myself that naivete.
Listen carefully while Chi offers further details.

Yet in the flush of excitement over this thing,
I am still surprised at Chi's zealousness.
When he told me it wasn't Igbos because
I still had light fixtures and toilet seats,

I was surprised, but took the comment
for what it was: an insight into levels
of criminal expertise. Now he has this teaser:
"They will torture them proper.
They do this for free."

III. Building Flaws

There Are Rats

There are rats outside the window,
rats tunneling through tall, dry grass
that grows over everything you know,
rats you'd set ablaze with one scratch
of the match ending with your eyes,
that would squeal and sizzle the last
syllable of your name, would atomize
at the first lick of flame, if you could cast
that first stone into the primordial mess
of the courtyard the last tenants ignored,
if you weren't afraid to confess
to owning a first name the others deplore.
Rats that are not rodents, gnawing their way
from last letter to first, beginning your name.

Riot, Gwange Ward

There is a lunar eclipse.
In Gwange, the Muslim kids
pick up sticks and stones:
Allah is angry; it is a sign
to rout out the ward's harlots.

On our way to a party
whose x and y coordinates
in the Cartesian system we see
are the wrong place, wrong time,
we keep our foot on the gas.

Our car is a soft green grub
passed down a long line
of premetallic mandibles,
a nibbled bit of leaf from
a tree they carry on their backs.

Madman, West End Roundabout

Here where the sidewalk ends and
Gamboru, Baga, Kashim Ibrahim Roads
spill into a vortex of horns,

you pick up a scent:
old urine, old bush pad out
the perimeter of your fear.

Going to, coming from work,
we whites see you sprawled out,
indolent, behind the shadows' bars.

You yawn, scratch your balls,
sniff vaguely at the air or
study cockleburs picked from your hair.

The buzzing in your ears is distant,
cars and motorcycles are so many flies
worrying a long-forgotten wound.

Tensile as the silk thread of a spider,
a line of spittle hangs from your lip,
vibrates to your deep, resonant snores.

Bits of cola nut trapped in your saliva
will be there when you wake up,
feed your hunger fever with more caffeine.

Some have seen you rain
haymakers on passing pedestrians,
men riding tandem on their machines.

Like the cat that would rend feather
from bone, your limbs churn the air,
imitate the cops they call Yellow Fever here.

This is your illness, your private beat;
the roundabout, the Charybdis that would
flush the world of our annoying reality.

Your dreams circle some
carrion thought we cannot know,
find still water, safety, and sleep.

Foreign Exchange

for Karl McKenzie

"Is reason valid currency here?" you ask me, earnestly.
Your eyes tiny fists clamp around the small change of reply.

Say what you like. When all is said and done,
he who eats the head of a rat, becomes a thief;

the man who rests his head on his trousers
will dream a terrible dream: the dream that

dreams him the rest of his life. Time is the
open pocket from which mirror and money protrude.

Take what thoughts have pockets off the shelf.
Tell them to leave an inch for shrinkage in the legs.

Shooting Pigeons

Bang! Clatter, clatter, clatter...thunk:
the third stone rolls down the corrugated
zinc roof of my castle,
rousting me, a sweaty, angry Goliath,
from sleep. I sit bolt upright on my
terry towel stretched beneath the fan.

Neighbourhood kids after pigeons again,
only in the moments of half-sleep I think
of seagulls circling the high-tide stones,
dropping clams to crack their shells perhaps,
or of breaking glass, consciousness
a piece of paper wrapped around a rock.

I stumble in confusion, pull on my pants,
unlock the door, remove the padlock from its loops.
Storm the gates to rant about the windows,
snatch their slingshots from their hands.
This way, I point, away from the house.
Ba English, they say, ba English.

My syllables bounce off
the tin roofs of their eyes and ears.
The pigeons turn their iridescent feathers
to the sun, the grapeshot of their red eyes
spraying out from the obnoxious
blunderbus of my booming voice.

Ba Hausa, I say, ba Hausa.
The words, flung out in a slow arc
against the gold feathers of sun that
rustle, flap, settle themselves again
in the gnarled branches of the thorn trees,
the thin crotch of my only tongue.

Building Flaws

The new classroom wing
of the State Polytechnic
is finally finished.

Rebar and cinder block
held together with mortar
from head-carried hods,

propped up every few feet
with hand-hewn logs
and wadded handshakes.

Three floors, eighty blocks
for every forty budgeted
per bag of cement—

a child's recipe, the building
inspector will later maintain,
awaiting further ingredients;

a three-layer cake
in need of a little more
icing, a little leavening perhaps.

Perhaps a few more students,
a few more chocolate jimmies
sprinkled under mortar and dust.

Paula's Poem

Another assembly. All the teachers sit on a row of benches at the rear of the stage. You take a seat at one end, notice you're the only bature among them.

A school riot this time. One of the N.Y.C.s* has stirred up muck between the Muslims and Christians again. Broken windows. Beatings. Reprisals. And in the heat of it all six girls have been raped.

There follows an opening tirade by the principal. All the students are chastised for allowing anarchist acts to upset the smooth-running of College affairs. A litany of abuses is chronicled, followed by a catalogue of names. Ademu is singled out. Abdullahi. Mshelia. The Discipline Master smirks and fondles his whip.

Twenty lashes and three weeks suspension—a lesson to all students that shenanigans will not be tolerated. Bared buttocks. The sting of all those eyes like knots in the leather.

Your stomach rebels. You get up to leave.

Later you muster enough courage to storm into the principal's office. Three weeks for rape? Fifty lashes and expulsion for being caught smoking Indian hemp?

They're only girls, after all, the principal sighs, eyeing your breasts, staring you down. Only girls that should be at home.

* National Youth Corps

Out, Out Damn Spot...

It's leprosy all right: the open sore on Ndirmbula's wrist suddenly revealed like a watch face peeking from his sleeve. Hard to believe? Before you quietly usher him off to the principal's office, before thinking "unclean" though, think again. The bribe they call dash in this place pools like blood. Cash that graces a medical officer's palm may ultimately break out as a rash on a white face: your presence here—for which the locals are grateful one moment, angry the next—is a kind of wound too. You must take it easy. Save face. Make no wahala then. It's not a few shot spots on the white linen that need cleaning after all. Or the red stains on anyone's underwear in this play. Detergents with phosphates, antibiotics in undated bottles sent from the West make that level of morality come clean enough. You must confess: words are no antibody for history here. The spaces between their white sleeves come out grey, wherever, whenever we do a wash.

Karl's Cutlery

Ever since his bad bout of dysentery,
Karl has stayed away from vegetables
and meat cuts of any kind.
Pressure cooker or no pressure cooker,
bleach or no bleach:
he's not taking any chances.
Whatever he eats
has to come in cans.

"It's a diseased environment," he tells me,
meaning the school where he teaches,
the market, the streets,
the city, the entire country now.
And now he's moved on to more
elaborate forms of protection.
Eats only import items:
boiled rice, mackerel in tomato sauce,
and stores his cutlery in the fridge.

Every night now you can see him
pull his chair up to the door,
knife in one hand, fork in the other,
bathed in a glorious white light,
a single rectilinear halo
around his shoulders:
sitting in the one oasis
where he is safe.

Name Seven Wine-Growing Regions of France

I have a friend—or maybe he's not a friend—a colleague, or compatri-ate—a fellow expat who has become one of the people I will sit down to dinner with because he's Canadian and we have secrets, shared experi-ences we can break like bread and butter evenly. He teaches food ser-vices, hospitality courses for the hotel management program at a polytech and is a bit of an acquired taste himself. Not bitter exactly, but cynical and smug. He loves to tell stories about his students, especially the ones he'll tell you he has slept with or would like to bed. The naive ones, young Muslim beauties their families have sent to college out-of-state to catch husbands, who he's caught in their moments of weakness or inspired hope, looking for a way out of here. He's a liar and a thief, a man who cheats on a woman he just married before coming here—a woman ten years his junior, who loves him dearly and does not suspect anything, least of all the box of safes he keeps hidden in the garage. He talks of soaping himself in hotel bathrooms to lubricate himself. Of prostitutes who ride hard and mean in spite of or because of clitorectomies. Confesses to me past infidelities, speaks fondly of the time he was a sailor, hawked PX wares, duty-free cigarettes, while we ride his bike hard and fast between hotels and shabeens. I want to tell his wife his stories, but am compelled not to, not by reason of complic-ity, but because I have shared too much of his desperation, have sat too often on the back seat as he has listened to me. And I think this country has made prostitutes of us all. The stigma of white skin, a common lan-guage and culture is a bad debt we all have stamped into our passports. His need for infidelity is my need for this poem, or the next. So now, when he tells me a student answered his question, "Name seven wine-growing regions of France" with Champagne, Brandy, Vodka, etc., I understand the breakdown in translation. We are all naming wine-growing regions elsewhere because there are maps. We are all riding into the wind. We all soap ourselves for entry into another skin. To shed our white one briefly, as easily as we hang a coat on the door.

Expats at The Lake Chad Club

It is raining heavily outside these walls.
Besides, our windshield wipers do not work—
nothing does in these latitudes—not even
the electricity. "Ba light," the waiter says.

We are tired and want to go home,
but we can't, and that's all the doctor
wrote on his yellow prescription pad.
So we malinger in this colonial waterhole:

cattle egrets preening among the pied crows.
They only serve when we come and wait,
and so we wait. And wait, while waiters come
and go. The empire reduced to a convex lens

at the bottom of the tall green bottles here.
We wait until all the words of our witty
banter run in rivulets, leave a rust stain
down all our white walls. Our brains back up

with the fetid vapors and algae-green
thoughts that stand stagnant enough
for insects to breed in. And mosquitoes sit as
at a lunch counter to sup of our thin blood.

The dartboard on the wall holds no more interest
than the test pattern of the Indian in profile
we recall, thinking of similar nights in America
after sign-off and the national anthem. Electrons

buzz like gnats around the porch light of our dreams.
An agama darts down from the valence, having
spotted a fly. We have learned to appreciate
its statesmanlike nod. Can watch it for hours.

Our eyelids, like spiders, hang from
a thread finer than a bullet's trajectory
or the small, lead-hot tracers we watch
running down the dirty window panes.

Wes and the Doctor Bob Visa

Wes, I want you to know
your slow way of walking,
wasted frame and fine talk
have my head awash with
hope and possibility tonight.

Your fear over not being able
to get a visa, enough money
to get back in the country
from some bush town in Ghana
where a friend left you,

the way you lost your cool,
finally, back in Gashua,
scant hundreds of clicks
from the edge of the Sahara
where you were posted to teach,

and wrote about it and drew
cryptic runes and diagrams
all over your bedroom walls,
then wandered off to tee off
the edge of your map

into the biggest sand trap a man
can find himself in in this country,
playing the back nine for keeps
in a shifting pit of lies and deceit,
redrew the desert maps for us all.

I want you to know the joke—
the Doctor Bob visa—was real
for all your fellow batures
stuck in Gashua, Geidam, Nguru,
all the bush postings in Bornu;

that a little part of all of us
escaped with you and Bob on the plane,
while we laughed to stay sane
for one tour of duty or two
and sent our remittance cheques home;

that the final still frame,
the one image that remains
clearer than all the others tonight,
is of you dancing, one hand flailing,
the other holding your pants up.

So finally I can say Bob be damned!
You made it, Wes! We all did,
in spite of the caked shit
on the toilet that wouldn't flush.
You finally made your hole-in-one.

Wash Day

Doing the laundry with my feet—
so much easier than bending
at the waist, rubbing the cuffs together,
surfaces of the sheets.

Almost fun. My lungs inflate
as I run on the spot,
Omo agitates my shirts,
foments a heady romance.

Chin up! Chest out!
Those are grapes you're squashing, boy!
Think how much whiter
your skin will be

when you go home to
your electric washer and drier.
How clean the clouds will be,
how fluffy and soft:

God's crotch-stained drawers
suddenly seemlier, billowing out
above the factory lots,
the neighbours' emerald lawns.

Open Air Concert, Lake Chad Club, Maiduguri

Plush chairs circle the tennis court:
a plump, silk-suited arm around
the stalwart shoulder of the manager
whom they've come to impress, introduce
to the guests. We drink farther off
amongst the hubbub of knees and empties
in a covey of white picnic tables
that have gathered like doves in the farthest
branches of the trees. Neems, they are called,
though they remind us of Elms, fruit trees
as we count the dead soldiers gathered like
autumn windfalls at the base of each.
Dollars are being peeled from foreheads like
old bandages: great stacks of twenties sliding
from the dancers' cooing bosoms into hands
that take them the way the prehensile lip
of a horse would hay or a sugar cube
from the palm of one's hand; down the lead guitar
player's forehead, over the dragonfly glitter of
his jacket and into the road manager's pocket
while the big, fat bass notes bumble, careen
around the pistils of bottles, the corolla.

Man Must Wack Food[1]

Ba changey de taxi man e say
when I give am fifty kobo
for dis twenty kobo ride:

ba changey in de glove box,
dem coin rattle in his eyes.

Ba changey
counting de cash
at de big hotel:

no time for go to bank now
for get am disting float.

Ba changey at de club
where I go drink am plenty,
ba changey at de kiosk
where I go buy am bread.

Bakome, bahaushe,[2]
bature[3] sabe now:

bature get money plenty;
bahaushe no go chop.

Ba changey in de circumstance,
ba changey in de dance.

1. Nigerian slang, dating from the time of the Biafran war;
literally: man must eat (have) food.

2. Bakome, bahaushe (ba KO may Ba Hous shay):
Hausa; It's O.K. Hausaman.

3. Bature (ba TOOR ay): Hausa n. White man, European.

At The Central Hotel, Kano

For elegance, decor, and atmosphere,
the place is hard to beat. Indeed,
it ranks among the swanker restaurants
I can afford to patronize in my country.

I have it on good authority the cooks
can boast as spectacular a cuisine
as any my white taste buds have encountered,
and so here I sit, gazing at my menu.

I'm feeling underdressed, but not being
in a position to buy a suit and having left
my glad rags at home, I keep my eyes down
and watch my numbers: translate naira into dollars

appropriate the bingo metaphor while
I calculate whatever salad or hors d'oeuvres
I can afford. The local suits, their concubines
in all their finery, meanwhile, laugh aloud.

I cannot help but notice the sartorial splendour:
the rich brocades of their baba rigas and gowns,
the gold teeth, watches brought back from the Hajj
as class testaments to their Muslim pilgrimage.

Then, at one table, a statuesque woman—
hair done up fashionably in cornrows and beads—
sets aside her cutlery and stands. The gold
drips from her like water down an oar.

The handsome man's wife or whore?
I can't decide which, when in spite of her
beauty or poise, she gives the whole place
a decidedly different aura of grace:

As honestly, as matter-of-factly
as any peasant mama in the market,
she announces her intent to all:
"O.K., make I go shit now."

IV. Just Add Milk

Just Add Milk

An empty can we keep our pens and pencils in,
a label with the name of the product
arched in a capital-letter rainbow
—Just Add Milk it says—
above the smiling Reubenesque face
of the Dutch girl with the sheaf of wheat
clutched to her right hip, the basket of brown
and white eggs wholesomely hung
on the left forearm, crooked at the elbow
to receive the hand of her countryman;

an empty can on which her Easter-egg basket
hangs the cornucopia of her heart,
delicate fingers, red and white dress
with girl-guide kerchief collar,
cameo broach, white apron—
baring just enough flesh to be
decent, decidedly sweet. The lines defining
ample but not matronly breasts,
trotting out a country square dance
of invisible hands;

a can with a windmill in the background,
haywagon, horses, well-fed guernseys,
stacks of wheat that say production,
here lives Dick, here lives Jane,
the same smile that graced
cornflakes boxes, the fifties at home;
sensible-girl hands, wavy brown locks
that frame pixie-brown eyes,
white dumpling face, fluffy white clouds:
a vase of dead flowers we keep on the desk.

Petrol Queue

At some point we are not talking about depleted stocks, supply and demand, the stranglehold of the oil cartel. We are not talking of the need for new solutions, developing other sources of energy less expensive than fossil fuels. We are talking of two cops with billy clubs patrolling a queue. Of their frustration as they tap the leather of their boots. We are talking of stripes wider than tribal welts. Of the officer who loosens his belt to beat off the clambering hordes. We are talking of laughter as the man gets angry, tosses their jerry cans into the traffic-filled street. We are talking of a place where every second car is a taxi transporting bodies like white corpuscles all over town.

Traffic Fatalities

Where we come from
the roads are paved;
bodies break like eggs
onto a surface clean
as a Teflon frying pan.

Children stare out back
windows of their daddies' cars,
watch landmarks shrink away
like the blue turn-off dots
on their T.V. screens.

The moon we remember
ran like a car through the trees,
or stood like a nurse in uniform
above the spinning wheels.
We counted foreign license plates.

Here the children grow up fast,
if they grow up at all.
Call for passengers
on a bus that goes to market.
We count bones. The twentieth century
a matter of fossil record:

forty-four wrecks between Bauchi and Jos,
sinking like mastodons into the sand.
Kanuri and Fulani villagers
step across time, certain that
animals with such big eyes will see.

To the Peasant Women Who Stopped for Water

From the shanty town of Wulari you came...to the nearest standpipe that issued clean water and a prayer.... My standpipe...this prayer. That your buckets might be filled forever...and you find the journey less arduous on the way back. That the yoke rest easy on your shoulders...and the tin cans left over from some industrial solvent not rust out too soon...or deliver trace toxins to your children, their children's children. I would have given this much freely...only my miguardi has duped you into paying for it...five kobo a can...he thinks it little enough...and he brought you here. Five kobo to slip the chain from the big blue gate, let you flip flop in thongs, to uncouple the garden hose...

I was amused, of course...I didn't know. It was so quaint to see peasants in bold java print wrappers and flip flops...your rounded heels, perfect upright posture beneath the yokes. I welcomed you.... Bid you stay, come inside for cold minerals...and you did so, hesitantly. I couldn't resist: I gave you ice. So cold! So strange! Had to watch your eyes grow big, white as the fridge. I couldn't know the fire you felt as I palmed the cubes—so symmetrical, so hard—over to you. Couldn't know you would retreat so hastily...in fear of what? I did not know. Forgive me.... Come again. Leave the outside tap on—it doesn't matter. Standing water dries up quickly enough. Quicker than this ink running rivulets away from me. There is no form that I can give these words that will hold the shapes I gave to you. Please, stay.

Cockroach on a Lightbulb

A cockroach sits on a lightbulb.
Its antennae twitch.
How to find a crack, a seam in this
to brush bristles with the tungsten one?

Inside the bulb an insect intelligence
quivers to be let out.
Now on, now off, both round the globe,
climb a frayed cord to the ceiling.

Outside, crickets, frogs, cicadas all
dust the resin from their bows.
The moon is cordless, brother roach
they sing. Whirrr, Whirrrr...
Its light is all the light there is
and not its own to give.

Baobab

Stark as a ganglion
teased, razed from
the burnt flesh of earth,

the Kanuri say it grows
upside down in punishment
for an unweaned pride—

once thought itself
the most beautiful tree
on God's green earth.

How like a god, we think,
to invent an image
of such penury;

how like the heart's
dendritic branches
to hang its thieves in pods

while light like thought
seeps ever underground
to seek its deepest shade.

A Lei for an "A"

Dear Peace,

Just a note to say
how much I adored
your narrow hips,
jutting jouncy buttocks
and olive oil heels.

How lovely
I grew to find
your nylon-plaited hair:

How the distributor-cap leads
I saw in the design
of each carefully bound strand

provided the spark
that always
ignited your eyes.

A note of appreciation
after the fact
of a top button
done up on your blouse

to say
how I noticed your new shoes,
squeaky clean patina of black skin

the day you came to see me
and fell asleep,
hands clasped in your lap,
in a straight-backed chair.

How I really meant
what I said—
or thought I did

when I told you

to come over after class
for extra help.

You helped me
maintain some sense
of what mistakenly
might have passed
for dignity.

I wanted you.
Did you want me?

Photostat Your Documents Here

Kiosk, gas generator, and photocopy machine—
these and the right contacts in the Ministry:
a little dash to the right hands now and again,
and, in absence of "The Real Thing,"
the entrepreneurial spirit is born anew!

Copies: one naira (their buck) apiece, and steep—
until you learn: you can "walka walka wid dis your paper"
and wear out a pair of shoes getting the right documents.
One bature succeeds in getting an official form:
he duplicates it for the benefit of others here.

It is cheaper than waiting for the official
forms the Ministry "doesn't have,"
for the needed documents to suddenly appear
when the right lingua franca has been established.
And the more established the Minister,
the longer the handshake. And if the right
official isn't "on seat"?
A forged signature is cheaper still
and goes a long way.

So here I am, ready to leave,
thinking K never had it so good in Kafka's castle.
"Please, Mallam, can you help me?" I ask,
offering just the right degree of deference, a smile.
Flies taxi, take off from the countertop while my briefcase
grins, a somnolent crocodile, under the dinner gong of sun.
Watch Mallam's eyes float away like bottles
with my message inside.

"Come back tomorrow," he replies, the words waspy syllables
bumbling a hundred plump pinstriped bottoms that throb
over the single bite of their fallen fruit.
And "But Mallam—" I beg, right on cue,
this time with a little more gusto,
just the right mix of deference and desperation in the tone.
(In another week, or maybe a month, I know
I'll push people off the bus to board my return plane.)

"I've typed this letter myself this time.
All I need is the Alhaji's signature.
I know he's on seat. It won't take a minute..."
But I can see in his eyes I've mistaken
another forest for the trees.
A small bird, I have unwittingly flown
into their window, hoping to find purchase within.
My heart beats timorously in the cup of their hands.

The Worm in the Meat Is Also Meat

Oga, make you listen now.
Na cola nut e split two ways:
Na dis way, na dat. E na be so?
Make you chop, make I chop.
I tink you sabe, ba?

You go give me small small cola,
I go do disting for you, finish;
you no go give me small small cola,
for how I go chop? I no go do disting for you.
You go make big palaver, I no go talk wid you.

Oga, I tink you be teacher, isn't it?
You be big man. You go havam steward,
you go havam miguardi; disting, dat.
You go for house wetin be de air condition,
you havam big motor, you go get money plenty.

Dis our Nigeria, dis no be your country, ba?
Dis country e give you senior staff house,
e give you water, e give you light...
So how now? For why you make wahala here?
I no vex wid you. For why you vex wid me now?

Kai! You be stubborn man! You no havam ears?
You go pay me now, na you go pay dem plenty.
Is simple. E na be too much now! Kai!
You sabe book, e be big problem for you na
sabe "make I chop"? No holler am so-tay!

You tink I be idiot? You be idiot!
Na dis be one-plus-one now? Haba!
You tink I no go for school, isn't it?
You tink I no sabe dis your western
equality palaver, dis dem-o-cra-see ting.

I go for school! Den my fader e no chop proper,
I go for army for so. I make small small chop
for feed my family. I work am, I work am;
I no come rich for so. Dis cola make me bellyful.
Dis cola make me big man now, e na be so?

So no holler am wid me; I no go hear am.
Make you come back tomorrow, dis tomorrow e never come.
You go waka waka wi dis your paper, e never come.
I no go sign am, dem no go sign am.
Is simple. Na worm in dis meat, e na be meat?

Saving Face

1.

The fare from the custom's roundabout
to the University of Maiduguri gates—
a distance of some five to ten kilometers say—
is thirty kobo by van, fifty by cab.

The van is a Toyota Hi-Ace—aptly named,
considering the mayhem and higher stakes
involved in the driver making a day's wage.
The boy on the running board calls out destinations;
you catch his eye to flag down a ride.

Today, you must take your place at the rear.
Sit on one cheek to make room for the chickens,
their feet trussed, tongues hanging out in the heat.
A woman with a basket of dried fish on her lap,
baby snuggled in a wrapper at the small of her back,
sits forward in her seat, gold nose ring glistening.

You seem so neat, so prim and proper and pink:
smile, as the peasant women about you cluck
away in Hausa, nod in deference to their bature guest.
It is hot, but even so, the smell of sandalwood
overcomes the smell of dried fish and sweat.
You keep smiling. Watch the scenery slide by:
a strip of celluloid rolling smoothly over your eyes.

Eventually, the driver pulls over; you get down.
This time it is a mistake: he's got your naira note;
you're outside the van. "Babu," you insist,
"It's thirty kobo." Hold out your hand for change.
The driver ignores you, wishes not to lose face.
But you're no longer new here, so stand your ground.

When he refuses to cough up the money,
you snatch his hula—hand-embroidered,
worth at least fifty naira—right from his head.
Joke with him, "Not bad for seventy kobo!"
Tuck it under your arm, and turn on your heel.
"Come," he replies, and offers you fifty kobo back.

The village women have cracked up and cackle
to their hearts' content. This is a great joke:
the pink teacher is as wily as old Anansi himself;
they applaud your cunning and craft, visibly approve
of your quick reproof. Even the driver begins to smile.
He surrenders full change; you give him his hat,
that is that. Your business is concluded; he's happy.
No one has lost face; everyone has had a good laugh.

2.

But it is not always this easy;
the stakes are not always this even.
In leaving the city for the airport, for instance,
you may not be so lucky;
your driver may not be so cunning
as he is dishonest. Or maybe he's lean, hungry,
has given one too many white men a ride
to the airport today. You are leaving; he has to stay.

And so I am unlucky this day,
have begrudgingly paid a three-naira fare
and have thus laid myself bare to further abuse.
I have a ticket, a plane to catch;
the cabbie knows this is his ticket too.
He refuses to open the trunk
to release my luggage before he "catches" more.

And what can I do? I cannot call a cop,
or he'll hop in his car, drive off with my gear.
The cop, as likely as not, will want
dash—his cut of this action—too.
I can't take a swipe at the guy,
beat him for the keys, or reason with him—
appeal to his sense of propriety, decency,
though I tell him his cunning is piss-poor P.R.,
that I'm a teacher: have given more in two years
than I could possibly take from his country now.

So I pay the prick, though I
would much rather kick him in the balls.
I get my damn suitcases,
and, after two days of trying,
manage to get a flight in lieu of
the one I had a reservation for.
Push my way onto the commuter bus.
Watch gleefully as three
peasant women's bundles tumble
off the bus, smash to pieces, as we
cross the runway enroute to the plane.

Letter to Busi, On the Occasion of
Macing Her Miguardi

I simply wanted to say goodbye—honest.
I had some cassettes—rock, jazz—
party tapes I wanted to leave with you.

It wasn't late. Yet your family miguardi
had a woman, bare to the waist, on his mat
and your lights were out. Bad timing is all.

"Sannu da aiki," (Greetings at (your) work)
I intoned in my poor Hausa. "Kwal lafiya?"
(Meaning, Did you sleep well? as it turns out.)

Having thought I had been polite, extended the
proper greetings, I proceeded with my business:
"Madam, mastah—are they home?" But no:

He hustled me out your big blue gate,
even slammed it on my fingers.
And that's when I got mad.

I pulled out my spray bomb of Mace
(All those months of carrying it everywhere,
and I'd never found a use for it until then ...)

and let him have it. It worked too, thank God,
or Allah, or whoever was in charge just then:
He didn't have time to reach for an arrow.

P.S. It was fun. That's how bad it gets.
I had to push my way onto the plane too.
The view from the air is lovely though.

Heathrow

We are in a science fiction movie.
Steel footage reels out from under
our leather-coffined feet.

There are no mackerel tins here,
no fetid smells, soap suds,
standing green puddles, or garbage heaps.

Only things freighted with unreality:
chicken tracks of words, figures
picking their way across the video screens.

"May I help you?" is a battle cry;
a white-toothed smile: a picket fence.
Here they kill with elan and diligence.

Flying Home

for Gepke

Tastebuds seen through
an electron microscope
was your metaphor:
a picture you saw once
in a glossy magazine;

tastebuds on a small
section of tongue whose
attached palate of heaven
makes small dental sounds
against the milk teeth of
mountains I fly over now.

A small section of tongue
mouthing the single
syllable of "home,"
the long throats of
my hungry eyes
swallowing everything whole:

that was what the clouds
looked like when we left.
Returning to you now
after so long an absence,
I want to say "cauliflower,"
say all things are edible as light.

We Breathe Molecules of Leonardo

We breathe molecules of Leonardo da Vinci every day.
    —quotation from a children's science book

In Nigeria
the harmattan
brought many furies.

The remains of artists
and ancestors
were not the only
whispers on the breeze.

Expats joked often
of leper bits mingling
with less intimidating
molecules of tar
and nicotine.

Now you write
to advise me
the situation there
has deteriorated;
tell me of a week-long
killing spree.

Men women children
bloat, release
a more debilitating
more dangerous
evil in the streets.

A stench I remember
hits me here
as the cheap perfume
or diaper smell
spells recent evacuees
of the elevator car
in my apartment block.

Allah is telling me
to get off at this floor
and not the next.

There is a terrible
white light.
The heat of the Sahel
hits me with a vengeance.

I want to tell you, my friend,
that somewhere between here
and there a thief is riding
a cushioned pillow of air
that is the pneumatic
collapse of history.

We breathe in molecules
of Leonardo; breathe out
a white ghost that first
powered the sails to that
harsh grave of light.

There is a taste of
hard metal on my tongue.
Home and snow sound
like brittle old bones
crushed underfoot.
I am walking on air.

Not happy exactly,
but my attentions and intent
are attenuated, spread thin
enough among family and cares
that good thoughts can still rise
to consciousness.

I can breathe
molecules of Leonardo
and do not choke on
the leper bits
or funereal smoke
of white complicity
and guilt.

Home: Acadia Highrise

Two weeks pass.
Mid-July and still
I wear a sweater.

You laugh when I shiver.
Grow impatient with my
need to read billboards, bulletins.

"Starved for print," you say;
relate my compulsion to others,
though we both know it isn't true.

Two weeks, after six months apart.
I'm still a bature, have yet to
"splash down" in this hemisphere.

You are no longer an expatriate.
Have acclimatized. Can walk
past store windows with ease.

But in our new apartment
the bed remains a no-man's land.
We kiss and part as strangers.

Six months, and I feel
like a new N.C.O.
back on a furlough—

Only to you I must seem
a pimple-faced recruit
intent on conjugal R & R.

Off the pill, your body
claims itself a new
federation of cells.

I touch you tentatively,
recon with a rash of pimples,
other hormonal incursions.

In Nigeria an old blind man
—staff in one hand—rests
his other on his grandson's shoulder.

They go walking slowly
as you hold my hand.
I read the braille of your spine.

Acknowledgements

Some of the poems in this collection have previously appeared, often in somewhat different versions, in the following journals and small magazines: *Acta Victoriana, Afa* (Owerri, Nigeria), *Arc, The Canadian Literary Review, Carousel, Contemporary Verse II, Cross-Canada Writers' Quarterly, Descant, The English Quarterly, Event, Gamut, Ganga* (Maiduguri, Nigeria), *Germination, The Greenfield Review* (U.S.A.), *Lucky Jim's Journal of Strangely Neglected Topics, Luna* (Australia), *Next Exit, Northern Light, Pierian Spring, Poetry Canada Review, Prairie Journal of Canadian Literature, Raven, Rubicon, Samisdat, Smackwarm* (U.S.A.), *The University of Toronto Review, Watchwords, Whetstone,* and *Zest.*

In addition, some were previously broadcast by CITR (Point Grey, Vancouver) and a selection of the poems, some included in this collection and some included in the author's first collection, won the Literary Storefront Chapbook competition (Vancouver, 1982). The original manuscript, including some of the poems that became *Driving Offensively* (Sono Nis, 1985), and the bulk of these poems was co-winner of the Norma Epstein Award competition (Office of the Dean, University of Toronto, 1983).

My thanks to the various editors and judges for their support and encouragement, and special thanks to George McWhirter, Richard Lemm, Gary Geddes, Fred Wah for useful comments and editing assistance on earlier drafts, and to The Alberta Foundation for the Literary Arts for financial support.

Lastly, a nod to the staff and students of Advanced Teacher's College, Maiduguri, Borno State, Nigeria; Haruna Timta, Dr. Edward Strauch, Syl Cheney-Coker, fellow WUSC recruits and batures: teachers all—*nagode.*

POE/ST

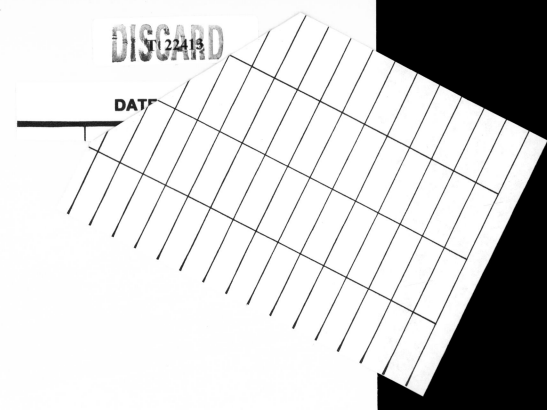